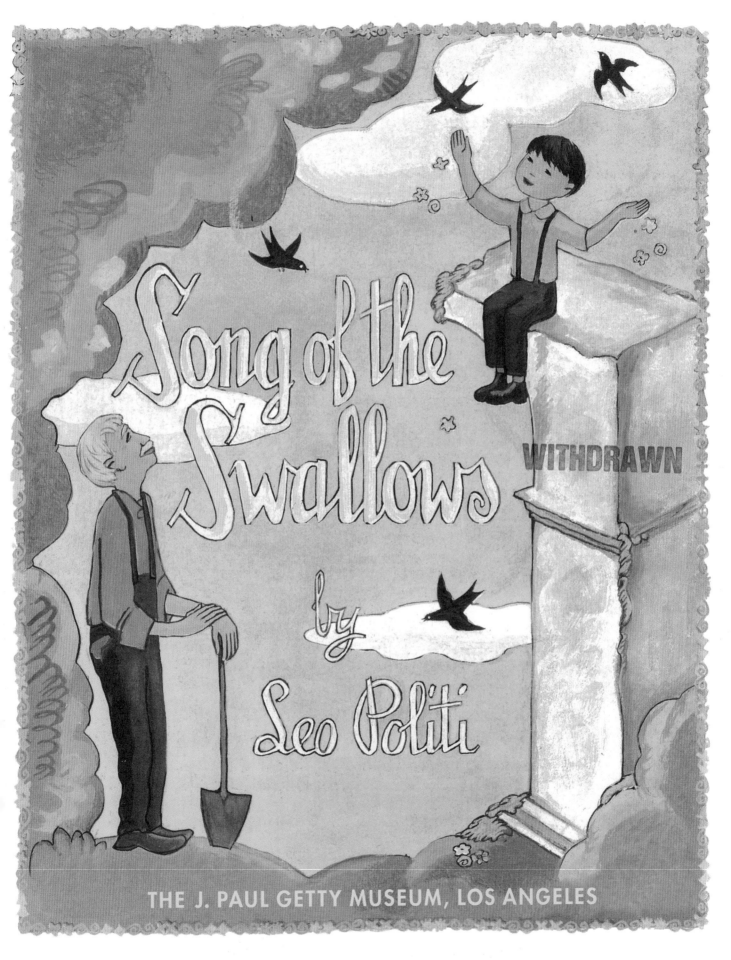

Song of the Swallows

by
Leo Politi

THE J. PAUL GETTY MUSEUM, LOS ANGELES

Getty Publications
1200 Getty Center Drive, Suite 500
Los Angeles, California 90049-1682
www.gettypublications.org

Printed and bound by Tien Wah Press, Singapore (W21237)
Second printing by the J. Paul Getty Museum (12906)

Library of Congress control number 2009924371

ISBN 978-0-89236-989-8

A T THE FOOT OF THE LOW and soft hills near the sea, lay the small village of Capistrano.

The bells of the Mission church were ringing on that early morning of spring.

Juan came running down the road through the village on his way to the little school near the Mission. He ran through the gardens filled with flowers, to the patio of the "sacred gardens." There he stopped to speak to old Julian:

"Buenos dias, Julian. Good morning, Julian."

"Buenos dias, Juan."

Old Julian was the proud bell ringer of this beautiful Mission.

Many times had he told Juan the story of the Mission, but always it seemed new.

"Long, long ago," Julian told him, "the good brothers of Saint Francis came to this country from across the sea. Father Junipero Serra and the brothers walked along the wild trail through the wilderness. With the help of the Indians they built many mission churches."

FRAY
JUNIPERO
SERRA

"That is Father Junipero Serra," said Juan looking up at the statue in the garden. "He is my friend."

"The Missions were like little villages," Julian said. "There the Indians learned to make shoes and harness, blankets and hats, tools and pottery—many of the things they needed in their daily life.

"Here is the big millstone where they ground corn and wheat."

Juan ran his fingers over the big old stone; he liked the feel of it. He liked too the little hospital where the Fathers used to take care of sick Indians, and the barracks for the soldiers who guarded the Mission from thieves and pirates.

On his way to school and on his way home Juan liked to look at the flowers in the Mission garden. They were so gay against the old walls!

Julian was also the gardener of the Mission. He took much pride in showing Juan the plants, for he knew and loved each one of them. Because he gave them such good care they grew strong and bore bright, fragrant flowers.

Many birds came to the garden to nest, for here they were undisturbed. They flew happily among the trees and drank the fresh water of the old fountain. There were humming birds, white pigeons, sparrows and other kinds of birds.

Julian always carried crumbs of hard bread in his pockets to feed them. The pigeons came and perched on his shoulders and on his hands.

UT THE MOST JOYOUS BIRDS WERE
the swallows. Juan called them by their lovely
Spanish name, *las golondrinas*.

There were hundreds of them nesting beneath
the roof-beams above the arches and their twittering filled the gardens with the sweetest music. They
made spring a very happy time in Capistrano.

"Ever since I can remember," Julian told Juan,
"the swallows have come in the spring on Saint Joseph's Day and gone away late in the summer."

"But how can little birds know when it is Saint Joseph's Day?" Juan asked.

"That I do not know," said Julian.

Juan was full of curiosity about the swallows. He watched them build their small mud houses against the beams of the roof. The female sat quietly on her eggs while the male sang his little twittering song to her. In the evening Juan saw them huddled close together, asleep.

When Julian's back was turned, Juan liked to climb the vines to see the nests and count the eggs, without touching them. When the nests were blessed with tiny birds, he liked to watch the parents feed the hungry beaks.

The best time of all was when the old swallows taught the baby birds how to fly.

One morning Juan and Julian watched a family of young swallows seated in a row on an iron bar across the arch. One by one the old swallows gave them flying lessons.

At first, as the little birds tried to flutter, they were so clumsy and awkward!

One of them tumbled to the ground.

"*Pobricito!* Poor little one!" cried Juan as he ran to pick him up. He held the baby bird close and soothed him.

When they found he was not hurt, Julian set him back on the iron bar. The little swallow seemed eager to get back to his nest. Perhaps he felt that it was feeding time.

One day late in the summer, Julian noticed that the swallows were noisier and more excited than usual. It seemed as if they were getting ready to leave.

"Juan!" he called. "The swallows are leaving us!"

Juan was sad because he knew he would miss them so much. He felt that he knew each one of them and they were like dear little friends to him.

The swallows rose, twittering, in the air, and flew toward the south. Juan and Julian watched, motionless, until they disappeared beyond the horizon.

Julian said, as he always did when the swallows left:

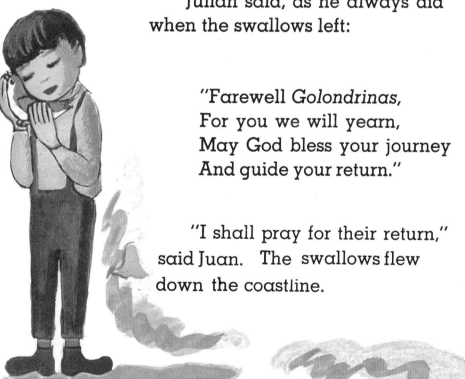

"Farewell *Golondrinas*,
For you we will yearn,
May God bless your journey
And guide your return."

"I shall pray for their return," said Juan. The swallows flew down the coastline.

"How wonderful the flight of the swallows is!" said Julian.

"Just try to picture, Juan, the hundreds and thousands of miles they travel, high up in the air, looking down over strange and beautiful lands.

I believe that, of all the creatures, God has given them the most freedom and happiness."

"But where are they going?" asked Juan.

"Some say to a land far south of us—some to a green island in the Pacific Ocean," said Julian.

"No one really can tell, but I do know, Juan, that they will go where there are flowers and fresh water streams, and people who welcome and love them."

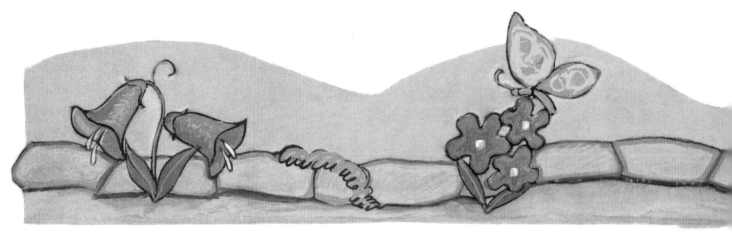

This gave Juan an idea. "People who welcome them and love them—I will make a garden in front of my house, then perhaps the swallows will come there to nest."

Juan's house was one of the small old adobe houses of the village. It had been built in the early days of California.

During his vacation, Juan began his garden. He had learned so much about it from Julian.

First he dug the earth. Then he lined the edges of the garden neatly with large rocks, planted new flowers and made the old rose bush climb the post of the porch. And always he kept the little pool full of clear water.

As the autumn and winter months set in, the colors in the Mission gardens became quieter and more subdued.

The Mission was still lovely but there was now a feeling of loneliness without the swallows.

On his way to school Juan often stopped and looked up with sadness at the empty nests. There the joyous swallows had lived and played, but now their little houses were still and lonely. Sometimes Juan hummed the song that he had learned in school:

La Golondrina

They'll call to me while passing in their play ---- they'll hang their nests— above my window pane ---- once more they'll tell me stories of their travels lovely winged swallows will return a-gain— Into my garden they'll fly to admire my flowers each little blossom— they will kiss in return— Once more I'll hear them calling to one another — my lovely swallows will return a-gain---------

W

HEN THE WINTER MONTHS were nearing an end, new buds began to swell and trees to bloom again.

Soon the blossoming trees bent gently over the garden walks. They made lovely patterns against the sky and filled the clear air with fragrance.

Juan felt he was going through an enchanted garden.

Julian worked hard in the gardens, for Saint Joseph's Day was coming soon. He wanted the gardens to look their best for the swallows' return.

The sky was tinted red at early dawn on Saint Joseph's Day.

Soon the sun rose from behind the hills and cast a golden glow over the valley.

Juan and his friends came early that morning to greet the swallows. The boys wore their best suits and the girls their newest dresses, with flowers and ribbons in their hair.

They played games, sang, danced and acted little plays of olden days, when the Mission reigned supreme over this rich and fertile valley.

As the gay fiesta went on, every now and then the children looked up at the sky.

Would the swallows come?

Hours of waiting and watching went by. Time dragged into the late afternoon with not a swallow in sight. The children became tired and discouraged. Some of them began to leave.

Then Juan, who was standing high up on the column of a broken arch near the edge of the playground, saw some little dots far off on the horizon.

"*Vienen las golondrinas!*"

"The swallows are coming!"

The children jumped up and down with joy.

The little dots came nearer, they grew bigger and bigger. Soon hundreds of swallows circled over the Mission.

Juan ran and hugged Julian. "The swallows are here! I thought they would never come!"

"They came late, perhaps they met a storm on the way, but I told you Juan, that they would return. See how glad they are!"

The swallows were very much like little folks who had been on a long journey and were happy to be home again.

They fluttered and twittered joyously and filled the gardens with sweet sound.

Juan and Julian went into the garden and rang the Mission bells to tell the people of the valley that spring had now begun.

The children sang:

Good Morn-ing, Mis-ter Swallow Come from far a-way

We are glad to see you On St. Joseph's Day.

Flit-ting in the sun-shine We can see you all

Build-ing up your houses On the Mis-sion wall.

Suddenly Juan remembered something and was anxious to get home.

"*Buenas tardes, Julian.* Good evening, Julian," he said, and hurried down the road to the village.

As he reached home he was happier still, because what he had hoped for had come true. Two swallows were fluttering about his garden. They had come there to nest!

That night when Juan looked out of his window, he saw the two swallows asleep on the rose vine. They were so near that he could feel the throbbing of life through their little bodies. He loved them, for they were two dear friends who had come to live close to him for a long while.

From afar, in the peace and quietude of the moonlit night, Juan could hear a warm voice singing.

It was Julian singing the swallow song.